Haidji

Ines' Words

Haidji

This book is dedicated to all lovers in the world
and beyond it,
to all who,
no matter what,
never gave up to believe in love.

Haidji

Ines' Words

Table of Contents

Haidji

The fresh winter air makes itself present,

bringing the scent of spring flowers.

The early summer green covers the forest,

contrasting with the red of the rocks under the water,

over which autumn leaves float.

Love, conciliating all four seasons in mid-January

at the Tears Fountain,

in Quinta das Lagrimas.

Haidji - Ines' Words

Haidji

Introduction

Pedro and Ines met in 1340, when she was a lady in waiting to Pedro's arranged bride, Constanca de Penafiel, a wife chosen by his father, King Afonso IV of Portugal, to solidify an alliance with the Prince of Villena of Spain.

Pedro and Ines fell in love with each other almost at first sight.

The love story between Ines de Castro (1325-1355) and King D Pedro I (1320 -1367) is one of the most tragic, intense and powerful in European history. Their story has become a legend and it is difficult to separate facts from fiction, where the only certainty that remains is the element of forbidden, but everlasting, love.

Pedro, forced to marry Constanca in order to seal the alliance between Portugal and Spain, ignored his new wife for the love of the beautiful Ines. This caused concern in the royal court, because Ines came from a powerful Castilian family. Pedro's father had tried to tear them apart by exiling Ines from the court, but the lovers maintained in contact, exchanging letters. After Pedro's wife died during childbirth in 1349, his father, King Afonso IV, became very angry when Pedro took Ines secretly as his common law wife.

The King, in an act of desperation, ordered that Ines should be murdered. Three assassins beheaded her in the Monastery of Santa Clara in Coimbra, Portugal, before her children's eyes. In deep grief, Pedro turned against his father and launched Portugal into civil war. The war lasted a year.

Pedro failed, but King Afonso soon died of a broken heart and in 1387 Pedro became the eight King of Portugal. Legend holds that Pedro stated he had married Ines secretly, although his word was the only proof of the marriage and he declared Ines as the Queen of Portugal, though she had been dead for two years.

He ordered her body to exhumed and had her coroneted at Alcobaca, where he ordered his vassals to pledge their obedience and loyalty to his wife and Queen and further demanded that they kiss her hand and swear their allegiance to her as Queen. Ines was now known as "The Queen who was crowned after death" or "The Death Queen."

Pedro hunted down two of the men who had killed Ines and killed them, ripping out their hearts with his own hands. The third, upon hearing what happened to the others, dropped dead.

The scene of Ines and Pedro's love is nowadays a hotel, "Quinta das Lagrimas" in Coimbra, and the Abby of Alcobaca is a national monument where the tombs of the two lovers lie side by side, as Pedro had ordered. Two tombs were constructed in the monastery where he had moved Ines' body, and he required his own tomb to be moved after his death to be laid to rest next to hers. Each tomb has an image of him and Ines respectively and they are positioned so they face one another.

On the marble of each tomb is inscribed "Until the End of the World". That is how he defined how long he loved her:

"Until the End of the World."

Over death and any political conveniences.

The legend says that Ines' ghost stills roams the Quinta, eternally searching for Pedro; and that if lovers drink together the water of the Tears Fountain, where Ines cried for the last time before being murdered, their love will last and they will stay together, Until the End of the World.

Haidji

I Berceuse

2020 – Coimbra – 680 years after after Pedro and Ines met each other for the first time.

The sun cast its rays through the clouds over the discrete elegance of the city.
At Coimbra's train station, Mariana waited for a taxi to go to Quinta das Lagrimas.
She decided to postpone the taxi and to have a coffee around there, first.

Coffee...she smiled.

She did not drink coffee before.
It was a habit acquired by missing him.
By the memory of the cup, between his hands.
As would the act of drinking coffee bring them together, taking him out of her dreams, closer to reality. She drank her coffee, smiling.

Thinking about how sometimes the intensity of feelings can make a little coexistence change the habits of people.

It brands.

Small moments that brand like fire-marks and seem to never pass by;

Eternalized in the acquired habits until they become unconscious, as if they had always been part of someone.

Arriving at Quinta das Lagrimas, the vision of the Place seemed familiar to Mariana.

The familiarity of a place wrapped in promises of coziness.

A Place we visited only in our dreams.

As Mariana went up the double staircase on the right side, from somewhere came a melody, "Berceuse" by Gabriel Faure;

While she watched the stone lion statue, placed in the middle of the staircase, changing his expression according to the angle from which she saw him on her way up the stairs.

In the reception area,
A blond girl and a brunette
Smiled, seeing her

And showed her the way to a room in the Palace.

Sitting on her bed in the room, she picked up her iPhone, but did not know if there would be an answer.
That's why
She just took it, and did not call anyone.

The wind,
which seemed to have chosen Gabriel Faure's compositions on this day to make her smile,
now played "Pavane" in her thoughts.

Cruel, the world in which she lived.
Where everything seemed to be more important
than love.

She opened the bedroom window and the breeze came in and brought a scent of perfume.
Mariana closed her eyes and inhaled deeply.
As would the fragrance touch her skin and, by inhaling it,
the scent would enter her body and go out again, as mild chills walked along her arms while she opened her eyes to see the forest.

Ines was running through the garden trees,
Calling for Pedro.

Mariana closed the window,
Brushed her hair in front of the mirror.
While in the mirror of time
she saw Ines
being combed by her lady in waiting.

The lady in waiting, she had herself once been,
washing his hair.
Mariana?
A long time ago,
where perhaps she had only dreamed about
to wash his hair.
And she smiled, seeing his startled eyes.
Amazed
because of such boldness.

She ran down the stairs, toward the forest.
The wind
played her favorite song, while drying her tears:
"Cantique de Jean Racine",

Was being played somewhere in the Palace,

maybe, in the music room.

Maybe, only inside her soul?

But... it was playing.

Haidji

Lonely duet on the high seas

Where are you?
        I won't say

Where are you?
        I don't know yet.

Where are you?
        Neither to you nor to the wind I will say

        Not to the wind
        Neither to the time
        Nor to the time the wind takes to pass by

Where are you? Won't you say?
Neither to the sea, nor to the waves?

        I don't know anymore
        I searched and I never found you

        I stopped to be
        I stopped to see
        I stayed on the sea
        And never found you
        I got lost

Between the waves of the high seas.

Where are you?
  I don't know anymore

Where are you?
  I don't know
  Not to the wind I will say

    Not to the wind
    Neither to the time
    Nor to the time the wind takes to pass by

Where are you?
  Now I know

Where are you?
  Lost
  Without finding you
  In the midst of the high sea waves.

Where are you?
  I don't know.

Don't you hear me?
I'm here
Asking
What happened to you?
Not the wind

Neither the time
Nor the time the wind takes to pass by
Allow me to forget you

Where are you?

I am
Where the moonlight touches the sea waves in mid-January under a starry sky.

Haidji

II The Swan, La Danse Macabre

Mariana ran through the woods in the hotel's garden, seeing her shadow running behind her.
As if she would be Ines, looking for Pedro.

She turned in circles between the trees with her hair floating through the wind, as would her hands be able to grab the time swing, moving backward and forward between present and past.
Singing and hearing her own voice echoing in her thoughts.

"Pedro?"

She danced at the entrance of the "Lovers Fountain",
Imagining red boats with messages ‐
From Pedro to Ines
From Ines to Pedro ‐
Like an SMS carried by water, by the sound of "The Swan" by Camille Saint Saens.
Mariana smiled, listening to the music in her soul.

Her iPhone?
Was left in the room,
in Silence.
The Silence that says everything by telling nothing.

Across from the "Lovers Fountain" entrance, Mariana sat in front of a tree. An old tree, very old, but younger than the time that had passed by since Ines' and Pedro's deaths.

The greatness of the tree took over her thoughts.
It was the "Tree of Love".
Across from the Love Fountain.
Mariana could hear Ines' voice whispering to her:
"To the end of the world, Mariana."

But... "Which World?" thought Mariana.

The tree continued taking over her thoughts, unshakeable, while Ines' words were fading away, echoing inside of Mariana's thoughts.
"Mariana...Mariana...Mariana".
As would the echo be happening inside the tree's root, as would it hear it, even if the tree failed to listen to ephemeral words uttered by unnoticed passersby.
When they stopped in front of it, few were those who did not fall silent before its presence.
The tree infused the garden's atmosphere.
As would it make all around it disappear.
Some people
bulged through its roots, at times when
they thought no one was watching them.
Admiring its strength and majesty.

Mariana stood up, and walked away.

Haidji

Sitting again in the distance to observe the tree,
One of Ines' love symbols;
That even the most intense storm wouldn't be able to overthrow. The love tree. Grown in the garden after Ines' death, its seed watered by Pedro's and their children's tears.

Being now watered by Mariana's tears.

Why was she so cruel?
The cruelty she had to herself
Only equaled Pedro's
After Ines' death.
The cruelty the world instilled in her
Covering her ears, to not listen to her own feelings.

"Pedro? Why did you become so cruel?"
She ran, listening to "La Dance Macabre" by Camille.
Running and turning between the trees until exhaustion,
She sat at the foot of the Tree of Love.
"Mariana.
Why?
Why don't you have time?"

Haidji

III The Arrival of the Queen

Mariana woke up in the morning and closed her eyes.
As if the perfume that she would like to be coming from his hands, touching hers, could not dissipate with time and could bring his presence back, out of her dreams.
She blushed and touched her face with both her hands.
As if they would be his hands.
The scent intensified.

As would he still be there. As would she still be inside her dreams.
She did not think she would miss it.
Miss the touch.
The skin, sliding under her fingers.
She inhaled deeply...as would that intensify the dream memories.

She opened her eyes.
He wasn't there.
Only air around her.
She went down the stairs, skipping some steps, almost dancing.
Listening to George Frederic Handel playing
"The Arrival of the Queen of Sheba".

Mariana went to the Tea Room.

She took one of the newspapers, sat at one of the tables and swallowed the newspaper's words.

As would she be reading

disjointed words,

letters where there was no sense at all.

She tried to concentrate and drank some tea.

The Muses' tea, accompanied by scones.

Where the lightness of the scones seemed to give the air she needed, in the moments she felt so sad that she couldn't breathe easily.

It was like to breathe the air

of his mouth, hearing his words.

She left the newspaper on the table

and left.

Her iPhone was ringing in her room.

Ringing loudly, but she couldn't hear it.

Haidji

Unexpected, was the touch in her dream the night before.
So were the feelings welling up.
As if time had stopped at that moment.
The moment between one word and another.
When new words come
and change the direction of the conversation.
Stopping the actual course of life,
taking a new one.

It's stopped.
Because in the midst of the apparent coldness,
Endearment appeared,
As the smile in the morning,
when her pragmatic mind had not yet woken up
to remind itself about her worldly affairs.
Creating caring Moments amid cruelty.
Because she couldn't deny that
she still remembered his hair:
Black, between her hands in a dream.
She remembered it,
while walking through the woods,
feeling the leaves brushing against her fingers.

In a world where everything was forbidden and immoral.
As if anyone could control or demand their own feelings.
Or as if time could kill them.
Time does not kill.
What kills feelings
is
Indifference, or fear.

Time just shows us what happened.
When we look only into the future instead of living the present,
Then in the future, time seeks and claws back the unseen past.
Bringing it back to us.

Haidji

If I Knew

If I knew what to say
I would tell you
Everything I want
If I knew what to do
I would do for you everything it takes
If I knew how to love
I would love only you
For an eternal moment

But I do not know what to do
I do not know what to think
I do not know what to feel

I'm afraid of making mistakes
Of hurting me, hurting you, losing you.
So, we stay like we are now
You won't like me
Nor will I like you

We stay just friends
Dreams stay just dreams
There is nothing to do

Because I think only of you

I like only you
But I don't want to see you.
I dream only of you
I speak only of you
I don't want to lose you.

Because life is just like it is
You won't like me
Nor will I like you
We stay just friends
Dreams stay just dreams
There is nothing to do.

If I knew what to say
I would say to you
All I feel
If I would know what to do
I would do it for you
All I want
If I knew how to love
I would love only you
Across the whole universe.

So, Good Night, sleep tight
Dream about angels and perhaps about me
Because I already dream awake
And when I fall asleep
I'll be with you.
If I knew...

Haidji

Haidji

IV Air, Prelude

Mariana entered the library with a certain veneration
regarding the books.
The books that still carried thick covers dyed from blue to red.
Keeping stories.
Thoughts of the past.
Emerging from pragmatic or non-pragmatic minds,
aligned in a romantic atmosphere.
Somewhere played Johan Sebastian Bach's
"Air".

As if climbing the steps of the library's rolling ladder to reach
the higher shelves would bring her the answers from heaven,
In a world of magic and colored covers contrasting with
wooden shelves.
Where only the black and yellow of the interior of the books
Brings colored images into the mind.
Transforming letters into images.
The heat of the images beyond the apparent coldness of the
books.
The heat from his hands beyond the apparent coldness of his
eyes.

"Ines...are you wandering everywhere with your presence?"
Mariana whispered, as she headed out of the library into to
the Chapel,

hearing the "Prelude" by Johan Sebastian Bach.

V Prayer

Low benches, lighted candles.
Mariana prayed,
while the shadow of the statue of Mary
projected shadows onto the Chapel's wall.
She prayed, with her eyes open.
Suddenly she looked at the statue
as would she be questioning it,
and saw the shadows.

A King and a Queen, two shadows from the same statue.
As would they be whispering while wandering through the
walls.
Shadows of sacred lovers created by the light of the sunset.

"Believe in deeds and not just in words.
In the acts we see who persons are
In words we see only
who they would like to be.

Believe in those who make you smile
and not in those who just smile at you.
Those will leave you crying alone
after you wiped their tears.

For as they did not see your smile.
They will not see your tears.
But only their own tears
and their own smile.

They smiled at Ines,
and then they killed her.
They ignored her tears.
They did not think about her children.
Driven by conveniences.
In a world where there was no room for love.
Her tears fell and gave rise to the Tears Fountain.
Love?
Love fell with her,
touched the ground, took root and was
reborn, as the Tree of Love."

Mariana continued to pray and with her eyes, watched the
shadows walking on the Chapel's wall.

Ines praying for Pedro in the shadows.
Chants of love, made by the last sunrays of the day.
Projecting kings and queens coming out of the same statue.

Haidji

VI Ninth Symphony, Moonlight Sonata, To Elise

The sun was on its way into the next day as Mariana entered
the music room.

She sat at the piano and played part of the Ninth Symphony
by Ludwig von Beethoven,

while the wind danced through the curtain.

She did not notice a man sitting on the same room, focused on
reading the newspaper.

His black hair called her eyes' attention, but her mind was
faraway from there, not following her five senses.

She also had not noticed him at the restaurant, where she
had eaten lunch hours ago.

Where the freshness of the water carried her to the fountain,
and the green of the forest passed through the glass, as would
it be calling her.

Shrouded in the mysterious silence of her thoughts.

Contemplating the beauty of the flower on the table,
that softened the murmur from the tables nearby.
Where nature towered over the talks.
There was a lawyer conference being held at the hotel over
this weekend; and he seemed to be just one more of the black-
dressed figures in the room, holding conversations on political
affairs, wrapped in the perfume of Ines' Words.
While the Death Queen was reigning in her eternal garden,
Almost imperceptibly,
the volume of the voices softened.
As the garden came into the restaurant through the glass
windows, reaching their eyes.
Where Ines reigned.

No, she did not see him, neither in the restaurant nor now in
the music room.
She played Beethoven's "Moonlight Sonata".
He did not move.
Just looked at her, until she stood up and went away.

The wind played Beethoven once again,
as she climbed the stairs;
The wind played through the hands of the man who sat at the
piano.

She fell asleep
cradled by the piano without knowing that this time
the melody was also being played outside her soul.

Haidji

"To Elise".

Haidji

Until the End of the World

Skins, touch each other
Even when bodies
No longer exist.

Touch me
With the skin of your soul
Do you feel?

I am in you
You are in me

Beyond reality
Love creates

Tears? ...Echo smiles
Pain? ...Echoes joy

Skins, touch each other
Even when bodies
No longer exist.

Touch me
With the skin of your soul
Do you feel?

Haidji

I feel
We are together
Beyond reality
Love creates

Until the End of the World

VII Adagio, Cantique de Jean Racine

The sun's rays came through the window, caressing her skin,
waking her up in the morning.
As would they be a breeze coming through the window,
passing by and soughing, taking the drowsiness away.

At breakfast they almost bumped into each other, somewhere
near the juices.
Not that there wasn't enough room.
The restaurant was bright and spacious.
It just happened.

Like it happens when people sometimes stumble by following
similar paths in the midst of many others, no matter how
much space they have around them.
Like an undercover meeting that can also be called a collision,
caused by the unconscious desire to touch each other.

Mariana went to her table,
looking around sometimes, through the room,
but she no longer saw him.

She wanted to see the Tears Fountain again.

She walked over to the fountain, listening to Samuel Barber's "Adagio for strings Opus 11", in the melancholy that the place caused her.

She stopped at the fountain and knelt down to drink some water.
She saw the red stones.
Tears sprang out of her eyes.

Hearing "Cry of Longing" by Augustin Barrios Mangore.
She felt cold.
All the cold of the world in which she lived,
Condensed inside her mind, to form the image of Ines dying at the fountain.
A world where conveniences were more wrathful than love.
"Ines?
Ines?"

She saw a tree that had grown like a spiral close to the Tears Fountain. Turning into itself, year after year.
To symbolize the Spiral of Time.
She collapsed, fainted; feeling dizzy, like walking in circles in time,
Seeing her tears mixing up with Ines' tears
That would turn all her sadness into moments of happiness.

Haidji

Slow steps approached the fountain,
Humming "Cantique" de Jean Racine.
Turning into fast hurried steps, as he saw her.

He noticed that she had not eaten at breakfast.
Wrapped inside her thoughts, so mysterious, so far away and so close.
Without knowing how to approach her, he had decided himself to walk in the direction of the Tears Fountain.
Where he found her, passed out, lying over the rocks on the ground, her hands almost touching the water.

He came closer and took her in his arms. Sitting with her close to the fountain.

Mariana opened her eyes and asked:
"Pedro?"

He took the water from the fountain and tasted it,
Before passing his wet fingers through her lips.

He picked up more water and gave it to her to drink.

"My name is Joseph, Ines."
He smiled.

Smiling back, she said:
"And mine is Mariana, Pedro."

Haidji

About the Author

Writer, artist, painter, designer, photographer, performer.
Just...**Haidji**.

Her interest in art began at the age of four when she got a
blackboard for Christmas. She then started to draw objects
around the house: chairs, tables, and so on. As she was
twelve, she started to write her stories and poems.
Handwritten and hand-painted books, for family and friends.

Haidji's University education was at the University of Applied Science at Idar-Oberstein, Germany, where she obtained a Diploma (Master's Degree) in Jewelry and Precious Stones Design, and Painting. She is also a qualified and awarding-winning Goldsmith.

Haidji is a talented and creative artist who produces abstract work that resonates with warmth and life.
Her stories create images in the reader's mind, as would each word be a brushstroke painted inside your imagination.

There is a very spiritual feel to her work, almost otherworldliness. A captivating blend of Brazilian flair, Teutonic precision and Dutch pragmatism makes Haidji's work unique, appealing and thought provoking.

Haidji has exhibited her work since 1995 and realised her projects and told her stories in many countries: Germany, Brazil, Italy, The Netherlands, Switzerland, England, Portugal, Spain, South Africa, Australia, Canada and the United States of America.

A personal note from Haidji, for her readers:

Thank you very much for reading my book.
If you enjoyed this book, please consider leaving an online review; even if it's only a line or two, it would make all the difference, and would be very much appreciated.

Best wishes, Haidji

Contacts:

Blog – **www.haidji.blogspot.com**
Email – **haidji@gmail.com**
Facebook official page – Haidji
Instagram – haidjiofficialprofile
Twitter – @Haidji

Haidji

14110617R00034

Printed in Poland
by Amazon Fulfillment
Poland Sp. z o.o., Wrocław